Fun with
Dick and Jane

GROSSET & DUNLAP • NEW YORK

Table of Contents

Look Up

Dick said, "Look, look.
Look up.
Look up, up, up."

Jane said, "Run, run.
Run, Dick, run.
Run and see."

"Look, look," said Dick.

"See Sally.

See funny Sally and Father."

"See, see," said Sally.

"Sally is up, up, up.

This is fun for Sally."

Who Is It?

Dick said, "Who is here?
Who is it, Mother?"

Mother said, "It is Dick."

"Oh, Mother," said Dick.
"You can see who it is."

"Who is this?" said Father.
"Who is it?"

Mother said, "It is not Dick.
It is not Jane.
It is not little Baby Sally.
It is big, big Father."

"Yes, yes," said Baby Sally.
"Oh, Mother, you can see."

Jane said, "Who is here?
Who is it, Mother?"

"It is not Dick," said Mother.
"It is not Jane."

"Not Jane," said Sally.
"Oh, oh! This is fun."

"It is Sally," said Mother.

"Yes, Mother," said Dick.
"It is little Baby Sally.
Funny little Sally."

"See my family," said Mother.
"My funny, funny family is here."

"Spot is here," said Dick.
"And Puff is here.
See this big, big family."

Something Pretty

Mother said, "Look, look.
See this."

"Oh, oh," said Sally.
"It is pretty."

"Yes, yes," said Jane.
"Mother looks pretty."

"Look, Sally," said Jane.

"Here is something pretty.

Something pretty for you and me."

"Oh, Jane," said Sally.

"I want something.

I want something red.

I want something blue."

"I want this," said Jane.

"And this and this.

Three for me.

Three for you.

Something yellow.

Something red.

Something blue."

"Look, Mother," said Sally.
"Red, yellow, blue!"

"Look, Mother," said Jane.
"We look pretty."

"Oh, yes," said Mother.
"Yes, Jane, yes!
You look pretty.
Sally looks pretty, too."

Where Is Sally?

Jane said, "Oh, Dick!
I can not find Sally.
Where is Sally?
Help me, Dick.
Help me find Sally."

Dick said, "Look in the house.
You will find Sally in the house."

"Look, Jane," said Dick.
"Here is something funny.
Can you guess what it is?"

"Oh, yes," said Jane.
"I can guess.
I can guess what it is.
This will help me find Sally."

Dick said, "Look here, Jane.
Look and see what I see."

"I see," said Jane.
"I see what you see.
I can guess where Sally is.
Now I can find Sally."

"Oh, Sally," said Dick.

"Here you are.

Now I see you.

I see Puff, too.

My, my! Puff looks funny."

Sally said, "Puff looks pretty.

Puff is not yellow now.

Puff is pretty.

See pretty, pretty Puff."

Jane Helps Mother

"I can work," said Dick.

"I can help Mother."

Jane said, "I can work, too.

I can help.

Look, Dick.

This is for Father.

Father will eat here."

Jane said, "One, two, three, four.

One is for Father.

One is for Mother.

One is for Dick.

And one is Baby Sally's.

One, two, three, four.

One for Father.

One for Mother.

One for Dick.

And one for Baby Sally."

Jane said, "Look, Dick.
You will eat here."

"Oh, Jane," said Dick.
"Where will you eat?"

"Oh, my," said Sally.
"Where will Jane eat?"

Jane said, "One, two, three, four.

I see four in this family.

Father, Mother, Dick, and Sally.

Father is one.

Mother is two.

Dick is three.

Sally is four.

One, two, three, four."

Dick said, "Oh, Jane!
You are funny.
You are in this family, too.
Where will you eat?
Where is one for you?
Now get one for Jane."

"Oh, oh," said Jane.
"Now I will get one for me.
Here it is.
This one is for me."

A Funny Ride

Father said, "I want something.
I want to get something.
Something for the car.
We can get it here."

"Oh, Father," said Sally.
"What do you want?
What do you want for the car?"

Father said, "You will see.
You will see."

Up, up went the car.

"Oh, oh," said Jane.

"See the car go up.

The car can go for a ride.

It can ride up."

Sally said, "Oh! See Tim!

He went up, too.

He and Spot and Puff went up."

Sally said, "Look, Father!
Spot and Puff want to jump.
Please make the car come down.
Can you make it come down?"

"Yes, Sally," said Father.
"We can make the car come down.
We will get Spot and Puff and Tim."

"Look, Sally," said Dick.

"See the car come down.

See Tim come down.

See Spot and Puff come down."

Sally said, "Down comes the car.

Down comes Spot.

Down comes Puff.

And down comes Tim."

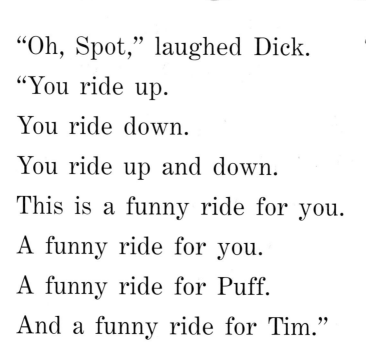

"Oh, Spot," laughed Dick.

"You ride up.

You ride down.

You ride up and down.

This is a funny ride for you.

A funny ride for you.

A funny ride for Puff.

And a funny ride for Tim."